This edition published by Parragon Books Ltd in 2014

Parragon Books Ltd
Chartist House
15–17 Trim Street
Bath BA1 1HA, UK
www.parragon.com

ISBN 978-1-4723-4279-9

Printed in China

Disney PRINCESS

Cinderella
and the Sapphire Ring

PaRRagon

Bath · New York · Cologne · Melbourne · Delhi
Hong Kong · Shenzhen · Singapore · Amsterdam

The Prince is throwing a grand ball to celebrate his and Cinderella's wedding anniversary. He also presents Cinderella with a ring with an enormous, blue sapphire – Cinderella's favourite stone. Cinderella loves it!

The ring is a bit too big and it slips off Cinderella's dainty finger. She quickly checks her pockets and inside her long gloves, but it is nowhere to be seen.

Jaq and Gus help Cinderella look for her lost jewel.

"Where have you been today?" Jaq asks.

"The first thing I did was go to my room to write about my new ring in my diary," says Cinderella.

And so, right away, they hurry to Cinderella's bedroom.

"No ring here," Jaq says with a sigh after they search everywhere.

"Well, let's try the kitchen, then," says Cinderella brightly. "I went to make a pot of tea."

But the only ring to be found in the kitchen is an old doughnut!

They hurry on to the music room, where Cinderella had been practising a new song on the piano.

Jaq and Gus search the piano, inside and out. But if the ring is there, they can't find it.

"We should try the library. I read there for at least an hour this afternoon," says Cinderella. Although they search way up high and they search down low, they can't find Cinderella's precious sapphire ring in the library, either.

"I also went out to the stables today to feed Frou," Cinderella tells them. "So perhaps I lost my ring somewhere in his stall."

They race to the stable and search the stall, but the ring is nowhere to be found.

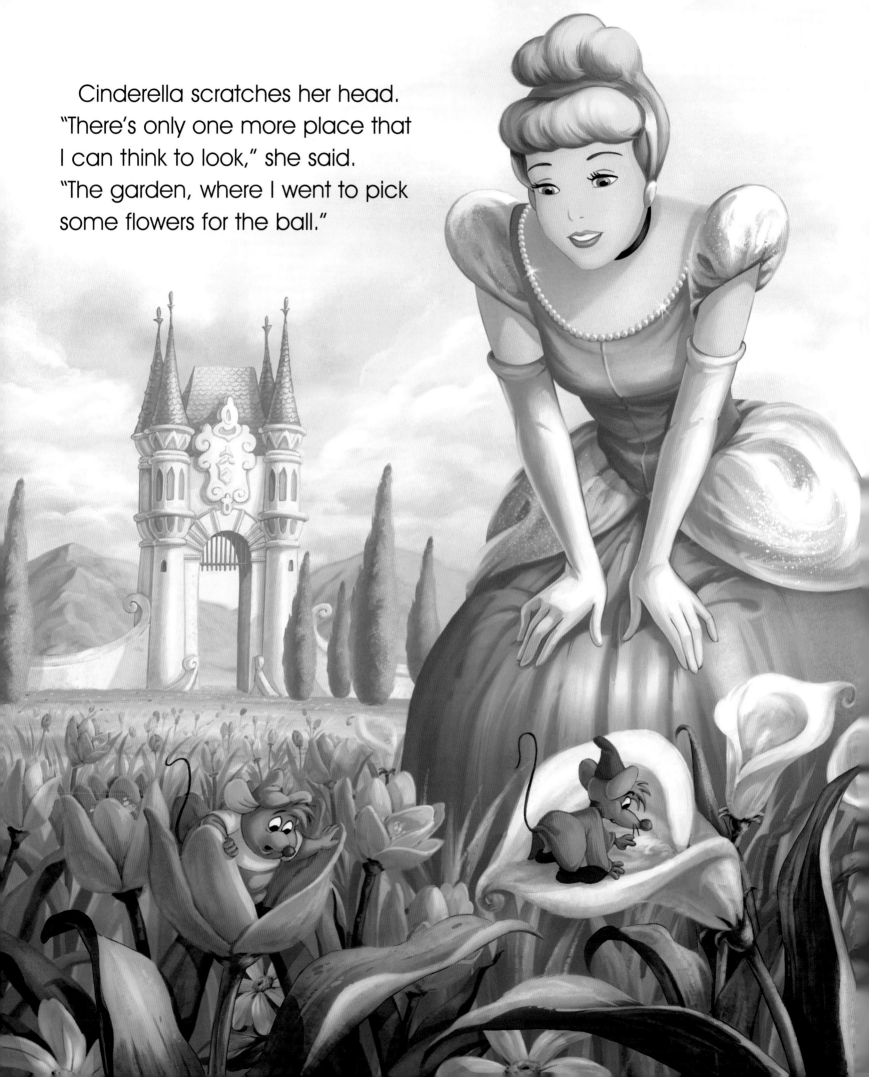

Cinderella scratches her head. "There's only one more place that I can think to look," she said. "The garden, where I went to pick some flowers for the ball."

They search every blossom until Gus exclaims, "Cinderelly! I see it!"

He scurries to the ground and picks up a shiny, round, blue object.

Cinderella shakes her head. "It's just a marble," she replies.

They head to the well where Cinderella
had drawn water for her flowers.

"I hope it hasn't fallen down there,"
says Gus, trembling.

But Jaq just rolls his eyes. "Oh, don't be
such a scaredy-cat. Get into this bucket!"

Cinderella slowly lowers
Jaq and Gus into the well.
"Do you see anything?"
she calls down to them.

"It's pretty dark in here.
All I see is lots and lots of – "
"Eek!"

Cinderella pulls up the bucket as fast as she can.
"Thank goodness you're okay!" she says with a sigh.
"Tell me! What did you poor darlings see?"

"Nothing," says Gus slyly, "but Cinderelly's ring!"

"My heroes!" cries Cinderella. "You found it!
And just in time."

That night at the anniversary ball, the guests toast the happily-married couple. But Cinderella and the Prince raise their glasses to their guests of honour, Gus and Jaq, and remind themselves how lucky they are to have such wonderful and devoted little friends.

Cinderella's steps to being a princess

1. Be kind to people and animals.

2. Share with others.

3. Always be polite.

4. Smile, sing and dance.

5. Keep learning new things.

6. Wear lots of glittery jewellery.